JACK'S TALE

JACK'S TALE

From The House on Fenley Avenue Series

Jeanne James Cox

iUniverse, Inc.
Bloomington

Jack's Tale
From The House on Fenley Avenue Series

iUniverse books may be ordered through booksellers or by contacting:

iUniverse
1663 Liberty Drive
Bloomington, IN 47403
www.iuniverse.com
1-800-Authors (1-800-288-4677)

ISBN: 978-1-4759-5597-2 (sc)
ISBN: 978-1-4759-5598-9 (ebk)

Printed in the United States of America

iUniverse rev. date: 03/05/2013

Much Love & Thanks to Kim and David.
To Davis. To special friends who supported and
encouraged this true cat tale!
To Miss Clara as my first young proofing editor!
To iUniverse.
And to Jack, Cheddar, Muenster & Jazzmin!

We hope you Love & Enjoy your pets.
Please adopt and support your animal shelters and pet
organizations.

Yea! XXOO

CONTENTS

JACK

A brindle-tiger cat. The smallest, most curious, and playful member of the 'Cheesers'. The Cheesers were three, very loved pets that lived in a big old house on Fenley Avenue.

Jack grew up with Cheddar, a pretty, green-eyed golden tiger cat—the first cat in the household!

Jack arrived on Fenley Avenue a few years after Cheddar. He was a tiny kitty with really big ears and *huge* blue eyes and a handsome dark brown and black brindle coat.

From his first day in the big house, Jack was a rowdy scamp, racing around with boundless energy. He lived every day like there was no tomorrow!

Why do you race everywhere you go" Cheddar asked Jack, shortly after he arrived in the big house. "Slow down—enjoy yourself". Tilting his head, Jack looked at Cheddar as he stopped to think about her question: "I just love to explore, and run, and why not go fast? It's the only way to be Cheddar" as he scampered out of the room.

One day a beautiful brown and white Collie puppy joined Jack and Cheddar on Fenley Avenue. His name was Muenster.

Muenster and Jack were partners from the start. A year old kitten and a brand new puppy—both about the same size! Two little guys in a fine old house with lots of love. Wrestling and playing like puppies and young cats do, they got along famously.

Everyone lived by very simple household rules—eat your food, poddy in the proper place, be kind to your people and each other. And enjoy life—it's always good!

"You are the fastest kitty I know", said Muenster soon after he came to Fenley. "I'm more than a kitty", said Jack. "I'm a whole year old, and that makes me a *big* guy"! Attitude was natural for this little cat. It was good to be the boy kitty. And great to have a cool new buddy like Muenster.

It was also very nice to get attention. Jack *loved* attention, and he was amply rewarded by every visitor to their house. When company came, Jack was first up to greet and enjoy the love.

FENLEY AVENUE

Home was a rambling 2-story house in a once fashionable turn of the century neighborhood. It was old, and often cold in winter, but it was home. It belonged to a wonderful couple named Brittany and Peter and their beloved pets they called The *Cheesers*—Muenster, Cheddar and Jack.

Cheddar and Jack lived in the office at the back of the home. The room had been remodeled with beautiful cut glass doors that afforded kitties a great view of the huge back yard filled with maple, dogwood, and magnolia trees. Muenster had his own quarters just down the stairs from the office where he slept soundly on his own comfy bed. These three had spent all of their lives around each other.

One year Peter and Brittany moved to England to work. It was difficult to bring all their pets so they left them in the trusted care of a Pet Nanny named Hannah. When Hannah arrived at the Fenley home, she also brought her cat she called *Jazzmin*.

Jack was highly curious to see who this new kitty was. The new guest was the talk of the house!

Who is she?" said Cheddar as she ate her breakfast that first morning. "I can tell it's a female cat. And I'll have my doubts if we will be friends."

I don't know" said Jack, "but I can't wait to meet her! Maybe I can cheer her up. She doesn't seem at all happy since she arrived last night. I hear her being so sad in her room. Maybe she's just scared of us."

She's probably never been around any one but her Pet Nanny—just spoiled that's what she most likely is" yawned Cheddar as she laid down to take a nap.

She'll be my friend you wait and see", said Jack as he curled up on his blanket to dream of chasing mice, his favorite food and meeting the new kitty. ©

A NEW FRIEND COMES TO JACK'S HOUSE

New surroundings are always difficult for kids and dogs and cats—at least for a few days. The new stranger in the house was a silver gray, long haired cat named Jazzmin. She was an 'only' cat, and very spoiled. This would be the first time she would share her life with any others but her Hannah—the Pet Nanny.

Jazzmin spent the first three days hiding under the bed in the downstairs bedroom. She was petrified of the other animals in the house, and she was more than mad.

JACK MEETS JAZZMIN

Hannah brought Jack into Jazzmin's room a few mornings later. Jazzmin hissed and growled. She wanted nothing to do with this boy kitty. Hannah held Jack as he stared at this new kitty in his home. "She's so pretty" he thought. "Hey Jazzmin, can we be friends"?

Jazzmin hissed at Jack, turned her back and jumped off the bed growling. She hid under the bed. She wanted *nothing* to do with other cats. Try as he might, Jack could not change Jazzmin's mind that day.

"OK Jazzmin" Hannah said, "you <u>will</u> get used to Jack and Cheddar and Muenster soon or you will have to live in this one room forever—understand?"

She carried Jack back to his room apologizing to him for Jazzmin's behavior.

His big blue eyes were sad that the new kitty was so hurt and there wasn't anything Jack could do—for now.

Jack just wanted to go back and get to know Jazzmin.

"Tomorrow we'll try it again," Hannah said as she hugged Jack. She tickled his ears, put him down and closed the door.

Back in his room, Jack ran over to Cheddar. "Wow, Jazzmin the cat is beautiful" he exclaimed! "She's also afraid of me I guess. She hid under the bed when I came in to meet her".

"Oh, poo" said Cheddar, "who would be afraid of little you—she probably doesn't like anyone but herself. I suppose I will be expected to greet her royal princess soon, but she can just get along without me—it is, after all, my house—it has always been my house!" Cheddar went to her soft cat bed determined to maintain her status in the house.

GETTING INTO MISCHIEF

Most every night, Jack's fondest wish was to sleep in the master bedroom upstairs instead of in his room. Like many little children, Jack was not always satisfied with life the way it was 'supposed to be'.

I just don't understand why I can't be upstairs", he mumbled to Cheddar one evening. "I could have *so* much fun at night, running up and down the stairs—the new kitty and I could run and play—and Muenster could play with us too! Why do I have to stay in my room"?

"Because you would be running up and down the stairs half the night" remarked Cheddar! "Humans don't sleep during the day like we do. Their only time to rest is at night. I think Ms. Hannah knows you will be the crazy cat that you are, and in your room is where you should be at night".

But of course, that wasn't what Jack wanted to hear—from anyone—so one night when everyone was put to sleep from Muenster to Cheddar, Jazzmin and Ms Hannah, Jack had his plan. After midnight, he sat and peered up at the handle on the door to his room.

He had an idea! He jumped up on the book shelf next to the door. He carefully put his paw on the doorknob.

Being a highly curious kitten—Jack was always watching people turn the doorknob and it opened the door! How clever was that?

"I just know I can open this door too" he whispered to Cheddar as he worked and worked with one paw trying to turn the knob.

The door didn't open, so he reached with his other paw—and jiggled the knob even more. "Just a little bit more—I know it will open if I just take my time" he grunted as he leaned *way* over to reach the knob.

What's wrong with this doorknob? It's not opening the door" he groaned.

Whoa . . . Jack leaned so far over that he tumbled off the high shelf and fell onto the floor with a THUD!!

In mere seconds, the door flew open—but not by Jack. It was Ms Hannah! Jack ducked back onto the lower shelf just as Hannah flipped on the light.

What is going on in here!" she cried looking at Cheddar and then around the corner to Jack doing his best to stay hidden.

Jack—are you trying to open this door?" She put her hands on her hips and looked down at Jack. "It's 2 o'clock in the morning Jack!"

He looked up at Hannah. "Well . . . uh . . . you see . . ." There was no way Jack could convey to her how much he wanted to be out of his room. He just knew she was very upset with him.

Hannah reached down, picked Jack up and looked into his eyes. "Now, I don't ever want to hear that noise again which means leave the door closed. You are to stay in your room at night OK?" She gently put Jack down, turned the light out and closed the door.

As luck would have it Jack had actually discovered an even better way to get out of his room. If he couldn't open the door himself, jiggling the door handle brought Hannah and once she opened the door, Jack was ready to race out the door as fast as he could!

Sometimes he was successful, and sometimes not. Hannah was just as clever. She could read Jack perfectly. A quick foot in the door stopped him short.

If he could sail through the door in time, he ran up the stairs to hide. He loved to hide. He hid in the empty boxes stored way upstairs. He hid in the utility room, under the tall bar stools. He hid under the couch, the chairs, up on an old table, even in the windowsill behind the curtains!

This was not at all acceptable to Hannah. Even though she chuckled at his cleverness, some evenings her patience wore thin, and she became adept at tricking Jack and catching him. Off he would go to his room. It was hard for her to get mad at Jack. But there were limits to his desire to not go to bed.

FRIENDS FOREVER

Over the next few weeks, Jack was never, ever too far away from Jazzmin. She realized how sweet Jack was and how much fun it was to play and run with him. It was new for her to have playmates. Being an only kitty has its drawbacks, so she got to know Jack, Cheddar and Muenster little by little.

ALWAYS SOMETHING NEW

As Jazzmin and Jack chatted on the soft bed downstairs one sunny afternoon, Jazzmin stretched and preened and delivered her infinite wisdom to Jack. "Now, I happen to have claws on all fours" she said. "None of my claws were removed—no pain you see. And I could go outside and if need be, fight off predators—you know, birds, mice and dogs!"

Jazzmin discovered early on that claws came in quite handy. A good scrape across a dog's nose sent a dog wailing and running . . . away from her! Humans quickly learned she had her boundaries.

With a lot of free rein to protect herself, she lived a safe and adventurous life indoors and out.

She described the various reasons for having one's front claws to Jack, including one she had mastered: "Now Jack, when one does not want to be picked up off the bed, claws in the blanket work really well" she said. "Just hold on tight when being picked up! All four paws with all claws out. Just pretend your claws are stuck", she told Jack.

"**G**ee, I could try that with my back claws cause my legs are really strong—grrrrr . . . just like me" Jack said with a proud grin. "I'm the strongest and fastest in this house you know".

"Of course" said Jazzmin with a wink.

THE HOLIDAYS

Jazzmin settled in at Fenley Avenue over time and life was good.

One day after Thanksgiving, Hannah put a beautiful red holiday tablecloth on the dining table. "How lovely", she thought as she placed an antique bowl in the center of the table. It looked so good on that red cloth in the dining room.

"Yes, this will be fine for our dinner guests over for the holidays," she thought as she left for errands.

When Hannah arrived home that evening however, and passed through the dining room—something looked off, out of kilter somehow. The antique bowl was not in the center but far over to the side of the table. She did a double take. The red tablecloth was almost on the floor. This didn't happen by itself. Wonder who should be addressed on this?

If she guessed correctly—someone had gotten up on the table, slid across it, and jumped off the other side leaving the beautiful bowl just inches away from the edge!

Just at that moment, Jack peered around the doorway, bounded into the dining room, jumped up on the table and reached a paw out to welcome Hannah home.

Looking directly at Jack, Hannah said "Did you do this?" Jack looked at her through those deep blue eyes, purring and happy she was home. He didn't know how to be 'guilty', his charm was in his innocence and carefree abandon. Who else would be so reckless on a dining room table but Jack?

"**O**h well" she sighed as she kissed his forehead, straightened the cloth back to center, and knew no harm was done—this time. All in all, Jackie was a very lucky cat. ©

WINTER

It's cold" snapped Jazzmin. She and Jack both lay curled up in the downstairs bedroom chair. They shared the French blue velvet chair. It was soft, comfy and warm. The weather had definitely gone to winter. Through Hanukkah and Christmas, the weather remained steady. Many parts of the country through the holidays had terribly bad weather—snow, ice, strong winds.

"You know I have been in snow so deep I was almost completely covered up—believe it Jack".

Couldn't you claw your way out"? Jack could not believe snow could cover you up. He had never been outside when it snowed. And claws were the answer to lots of things. Jack had claws only on his back feet but it never made a difference to he or Cheddar.

Jazzmin rolled her eyes. "You don't claw your way out of snow silly. It's like frozen water. Just wait, you'll get to go out and see snow for yourself this winter I'll bet". The concept of water you drink becoming snow puzzled Jack. He couldn't wait til it snowed!

JACK AND SNOW!

Snow! It fell on the patio, it landed softly on the tree limbs, and blanketed the ground.

"Wow—it's snowing. I gotta tell Jazzmin" shouted Jack as he pressed his nose up against the cold window pane in his room. He turned and ran out of his room to find her. "Jazzmin, Jazzmin—it's snowing!" He was so excited he flew onto Jazzmin's bed, almost landing on her. "Are you going out"?

Jazzmin looked out her window—"well, I certainly can't go anywhere until Miss Hannah comes home Jack. Besides, my soft fur gets so wet with snow—it has to be dried with a hair drier you know. So, I'm not sure".

"Oh please go out so I can go too!" Jack was beside himself this year—he looked forward to snow.

"Tell you what" said Jazzmin. "I'll get Ms Hannah to let me out on the back steps and hopefully you can go on out to the patio and be in snow yourself".

"Cool", said Jack—another adventure!

When Hannah arrived home Jazzmin sat at the patio doors waiting to be let out. "You really want to go out?" said Hannah. Jazzmin pawed at the door and looked up. "OK, it is snow and remember, it's wet". Jazzmin looked around and Jack was waiting for his chance to go out. "Jack, do you want to go out in the snow?"

At that moment she opened the door—Jazzmin gingerly stepped out on to the first step just as Jack bailed out behind her landing in the snow at the bottom of the steps.

He jumped up realizing how cold the snow really was.

"**Brrrrr** . . . Jazzmin this is COLD" he shouted. Jack picked up his front paw and tried to shake the snow off, then he shook the other paw.

Jazzmin laughed "it's impossible to shake it off Jack—you'll just get more snow on your paws".

Jack began to jump through the snow. "This is awesome Jazzmin—wow I didn't know snow could be so wet" He bounded through the cold snow wanting to stay out forever. Jazzmin, however, was ready to retreat back into the house.

Hannah opened the door. Jazzmin went in as Jack scrambled into the laundry room where he was immediately stopped. "Now Jack," said Hannah, "the one rule of going out in the snow—is coming back in and getting dried off". She grabbed a soft warm towel and picked Jack up to dry his paws. It felt sooo good. Jack had been in snow—he <u>loved</u> it!

THE BIG YARD

The house on Fenley had a huge yard surrounded by a 6-foot high wooden fence. Even Muenster couldn't get out of this yard as big as he was. At 80 pounds, he had grown to be a tall, handsome collie dog. The fence was built mainly for Muenster to have the full run of the yard—to get his exercise and chase the squirrels up the huge trees. Tons of squirrels lived in the many tall oak, maple, and pine trees that surrounded the yard.

When Jazzmin came to live at Fenley Avenue, she was delighted to find a big yard to explore. She was also adept at chasing squirrels up their trees. Squirrels were often the same size as Jazzmin, so the chase was always in fun and good running pursuit.

After Jack's foray in the winter snow, he stayed inside til spring. But one day Hannah decided it would be OK for Jack to go out just a little bit—if he stayed close and on the patio. "Jack do you want to go out in back with me?" she called.

No need to be asked twice, it was spring and he walked out and it took his little breath away. The wind was gently blowing—squirrels were scampering, birds sang, leaves were swaying in the enormous trees, the sun was shining. Jack Walked down the steps onto the patio.

He looked all around. He looked up—waaay up into the very tall trees. He looked out to the far back of the yard where the tall wooden fence separated his yard with the neighbors. "Oh my gosh what a big world there is out here" It all looked so different from the snow yard-bigger even!

Jack began to walk slowly around the patio table and chairs. Without the snow, he could easily walk across the wide patio, and then out onto the grass. He ran toward a large gray squirrel poised at the bottom of the big maple tree. The squirrel eyed Jack—chattering at him. With no fear, Jack ran toward the squirrel. "Hi squirrel—I'm Jack, and I'm out in the yard for the first time since the snow!"

The squirrel squinted at Jack. "You don't look so familiar out here in the yard Jack" she said. "Where have you been all this time? We're here all year around—living up in that tree you see. We know everyone at your house—Muenster and Jazzmin. I've even seen you and Cheddar at the windows—fancy you are now going outside?"

It's my second time out!" said Jack just as Ms Hannah came close enough to shoo away Ms Squirrel. "Jack—you can't just go up to a squirrel—they might bite you" she said.

"Oh no—she was a really nice squirrel" he thought as Hannah scooped him up and carried him back to the patio.

"Jack you can have fun but only stay out briefly. I don't know if you're ready to be out here alone" Hannah said. "Let's let Muenster and Jazzmin out too".

She opened the back door and out bounded Muenster racing past Jack. "Isn't this the best Jack?" he said as he practically galloped out into the yard. Muenster turned and stopped—looking for Jack to run with him. Off Jack went—running and stopping to look, and running and well, just pure bliss and delight was all he could feel!

Wheee . . . this is great!" he cried as he ran past Muenster. Together they raced around the yard. Jack ran so fast—if he couldn't outrun Muenster, he could almost outmaneuver him as they ran down the big yard and around the slope and back up around the apple tree.

Hannah watched from the steps—it *was* total delight seeing them play together outdoors. Jazzmin did not join in the running—she could run fast too, but for now she lay down in the lovely sun on the patio and stretched to enjoy herself.

MUENSTER
THE HERDING DOG

Over the next few years life was fine on Fenley Avenue. Jack was accorded the privilege of going out in the back yard.

The Rules of going outside, however, were always broken when Jack was involved.

As it so happened, he was just small enough to wiggle through part of the wooden fence on the far side of the garage. A little ditch ran along side the garage near the wood pile that separated Jack's property from the neighbors.

The first time he escaped the yard, Hannah had gone into the house for only a few minutes. She came back out and couldn't for the life of her see Jack anywhere in the yard. Where in the world did he go she said to herself.

She went all around the yard—looking under a large pile of tree branches that had fallen from a winter ice storm. She peered into every broken space in the wooden fence.

She opened the big gate and went up and down the driveway and front yard.

Oh dear, he's not used to being out by himself. Now what do I do!" Muenster had been tagging along with her wondering why she was so worried. She turned and looked at this big saddle tan and white pony of a collie dog. "Muenster I don't suppose YOU know where Jack is?"

With a smile that never left his face—Muenster practically said "I can find him!" They hurried back to the patio.

Muenster—go find Jack! Go on—go find Jack. Where's Jack?" she commanded as she pointed toward the back yard. Muenster looked toward the yard and took off in a flash—heading all the way to the back fence. Within seconds—he picked up Jack's scent and ran down the slope to the back of the garage.

Since he was way too big to get under the fence like Jack, Hannah called him back to the patio and they went out of the gate to the other side of the garage by the neighbor's fence.

"Where's Jack?" Hannah said as she looked at Muenster.

Muenster stepped down into the small ditch and walked a few yards to a large palette leaning against the garage. Hannah stepped down into the small pathway to where Muenster stood, smiling as usual.

She peered behind the palettes. There was Jack—little Jack hiding behind the palettes hoping he wouldn't be discovered!

Jack—you get out of there NOW"! Jack ran with glee past the wood pile and across the drive way, followed closely by Muenster as he herded Jack through the gate into the back yard. Jack could hardly stop he was so excited.

Muenster sat on the patio panting and smiling. He had done his job. "Good boy Muenster—you are truly a herding dog!" she laughed! "I think I've found the answer to finding Jack".

Then she turned to Jack—"Little boy—you are not to hide from me again-understand?"

There would be numerous times he would sneak out of the yard and hide, and it was always Muenster who found him, running behind him, herding him back to the house. Muenster loved his new role!

NOVEMBER

Late in the evening, as she cleaned the house after having friends over, Hannah reached down and picked Jack up to put him in his room. His lightness puzzled her. Then it startled her! He was so thin! "How did you get so thin Jack"?

Jack couldn't really think how, he just knew something hurt in him and he couldn't find a way to tell her. Losing weight was just happening. He was eating, but something inside his little body was not quite right.

Jackie we're going to the doctor tomorrow morning". Jack loved Dr. Gray and his staff. He went every year for his annual exam, and of course, always came away as a healthy kitty.

The next morning, Hannah bundled Jack into his blue carrier and put him in her truck. Jack didn't mind the ride. He liked the vet's office.

He wasn't prepared however, for having his neck shaved so they could take blood and test it.

Yuk" Jack thought when they finished drawing blood. The place on his neck where they shaved him to sample his blood hurt a little. "Hope we don't have to do this again soon" he winced.

It wasn't long before she knew. The phone call the next day spelled it out. Jack's kidney's were failing. "Oh no" she said. "What do I do? Can we give him shots or pills?" "No, it's not that easy" said Dr. Gray. "We need to get his weight back up. He's lost 3 pounds. On a nine pound cat, that's 1/3 of his weight"

Oh dear, do we know how long it will take for Jack to heal?

"It's too hard to make a decision on that" Dr. Gray explained. "Getting his weight back with the proper food can help him so much in the long run. He's been a healthy boy, and we'll try to keep him going for a long, long time".

LATER THAT DAY

Hannah held Jack for a long time that evening. He seemed so tired after the tests and being confined most of the day at the vet's office. She stroked his little body, promised him she would do everything she could to get him back to wellness. She gently put Jack down in his room.

Over the next week, she spoon fed Jack soft kitty food and gave him lots of water with a liquid dropper. It wasn't easy.

Jack didn't like soft kitty food and having water squirted in his mouth was gross—not at all pleasant, he thought. But life is full of changes.

Jazzmin sat in her blue chair in the bedroom eyeing Jack the next day. "Kinda rough going isn't it Jack? I feel for you and wish I could help. Tell you what, I'll break my own personal rules and share all <u>my</u> food with you!"

"That's OK," said Jack. I'm not real hungry now. Maybe I'll eat more later. But thanks, I like eating from your bowl. It's always good food."

The vet sent Jack home with a big bag of new cat food designed just for kitties with kidney problems. Hannah decided Jack's new food plus Jazzmin's food and Cheddar's food would all be shared with Jack. He could eat whatever he wanted, and as much as he wanted—he really needed to gain his weight up.

Hannah praised Jack when he ate, and made sure he had plenty of food and water. It didn't get past her that Jazzmin was allowing him to eat from *her* bowl.

This is a very good thing to happen, and highly unusual, she thought. Jazzmin wasn't known to be generous. What was hers was hers. But even Jazzmin learned that sharing worked both ways. She gained wonderful friends on Fenley Avenue and a real best friend with Jack.

Jazzmin, I just don't have the strength to play like we used to" Jack said one day. He had been playing with Jazzmin for over three years, and they had been having the time of their lives. But he was growing tired.

"Jack, no one expects you to keep up all that energy you have always had". "Besides, I myself am getting on in years you know, and rough play for me is not as often as it used to be".

It seems that cats sense a life that is growing dim. Kidneys are vital to keeping the body clean and flushing out the toxins—or the impurities the body carries. Jazzmin's role was now to build Jack's confidence and praise him for the great kitty he has always been.

A LONG LIFE
FOR JACK THE CAT

One evening, Jazzmin and Jack were lying on the upstairs bed. Jack had been having a tough time walking and getting comfortable that day. His little body had lost a bit more weight and he just didn't feel so good.

Jack said softly to Jazzmin "I just don't feel good today". Jazzmin leaned over toward Jack. With a natural ability, she could smell the toxins and sensed his pain.

"Jack, the one thing we animals know better than humans, is the time to live life to the fullest and know when it's time to go. You have had a long life and a *Fun* life! Everyone likes you".

"You're my best friend. I'm so glad we've spent this long time together Jack. If you hurt, maybe it's time to go".

Jack nodded his little head. He was tired. "Jazzmin, you have been a great teacher. I enjoy being around you. With you and Muenster and Cheddar, I couldn't be a luckier cat, don't you think?"

Jazzmin reached out with her paw and gently touched Jack's paw.

Jack felt at peace and very, very loved in the house on Fenley Avenue.

AUTHOR'S NOTE

That night Jack sat on the arm of the couch while Hannah read. She closed her book and picked Jack up. It was time for everyone to go to bed. And Jack needed to go to his room.

As she carried Jack through the dining room, he tried as always to resist going to his room. This night was different.

Suddenly he began to purr very loud, and Hannah was startled. It was a sound of a thousand purrs.

She held him up, perplexed at what was happening. As she neared his room, Jack took one long breath and then he sighed a long low deep sigh.

He died gently in her arms.

*   *   *

Jack's grave is on the knoll that overlooks the shady back yard and the big house he grew up in, a place he loved and a home where everyone loved **Jack the Cat**.

Printed in the United States
By Bookmasters